DOW/CH

We hope you enjoy this book.
Please return or renew it by the due date.
You can renew it at **www.norfolk.gov.uk/libraries**
or by using our free library app. Otherwise you can
phone **0344 800 8020** - please have your library
card and pin ready.
You can sign up for email reminders too.

10/20

HODDER CHILDREN'S BOOKS

First published in Great Britain in 2020 by Hodder Children's Books

1 3 5 7 9 10 8 6 4 2

A CIP catalogue record for this book
is available from the British Library.

ISBN 978 1 444 95 165 3

Printed and bound in Great Britain

The paper and board used in this book are
made from wood from responsible sources.

MIX
Paper from
responsible sources
FSC® C104740

Hodder Children's Books
An imprint of Hachette Children's Group
Part of Hodder and Stoughton
Carmelite House
50 Victoria Embankment
London EC4Y 0DZ

An Hachette UK Company
www.hachette.co.uk
www.hachettechildrens.co.uk

For...  + +

CHAPTER ONE

OK, so before I start chatting there are some people you should know about.

First, there's me, **Molly Mills**...

AGE: 9 years old

LIKES: doodling and collecting pencil toppers
(so far, I have seven)

DISLIKES: spelling tests and leaky yoghurt
(more on that later)

1

Next, there's my best friend,

Chloe Trout...

AGE: 9 years old

LIKES: peanut butter milkshakes (I like those too) and space stuff (she wants to go to Mars but I think she'd miss milkshakes too much)

OFFICIAL MEMBER
PEANUT BUTTER
MILKSHAKE
FAN CLUB
Chloe Trout

DISLIKES:

cheese and onion burps

(it only happened once and I said sorry)

And then there's **MR STILTON**.

AGE: unknown
(but Chloe thinks he looks older than our mums and dads)

LIKES: stinky coffee, beards and spelling tests

DISLIKES: us

BEST TEACHER

huh?!?

3

Really, I don't think Mr Stilton likes us. And I'm not the only one who thinks that. Chloe agrees with me. She thinks he's one of those greedy teachers who's only in it for the money. She says when he's rich from teaching he'll probably buy a private island. Then he can ban kids altogether.

Anyway, there's more people you should know about but I want to get started.

So let's talk about Monday.

Mr Stilton is always a bit moody, but this Monday he was worse than ever. We were meant to be planning our pirate stories. You know the sort of thing I mean:

Name: blah blah blah blah
Title: blah blah blah blah blah blah

Beginning: blah blah blah blah blah blah blah

Middle: blah blah blah blah blah blah blah

End: blah blah blah blah blah

← (Except with story ideas, not blah blah.)

And Mr Stilton was really grouchy about it.

"Silence, snottlings!" he said, or something like that. "You will write your story plans. You will write *beautifully*. And you will write quietly."

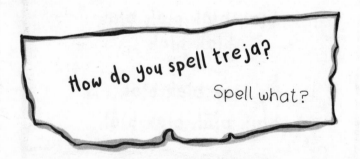

Well I couldn't write *beautifully* because I was stuck for ideas. So I wrote Chloe a note instead.

How do you spell treja?

Spell what?

Treja.

I don't know that word. Are you
sure you're spelling it right?

No?!?!?

Geez, calm down. I've got stuff
on my mind. What does it mean?

Gold and stuff. Coins? Gems?

Oh. No. Sorry. Don't know it.
BTW have you seen how
much Emily's written?

Let me explain about **Emily**.

Emily is really good at everything.

She speaks like four languages or something and

she plays piano and flute and bassoon
(which, it turns out, is not
a kind of monkey).

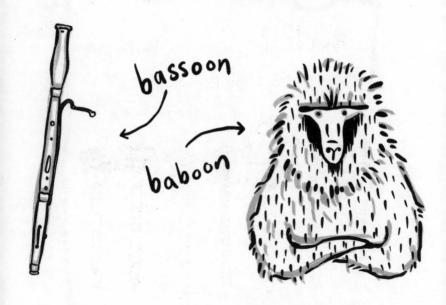

bassoon

baboon

And she's got **fourteen** pencil toppers.

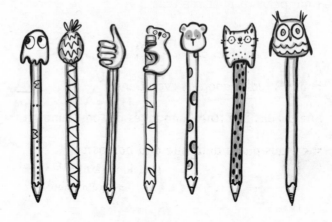

That's twice as many as me. Not that I'm jealous.

Well, maybe just a little bit.

Everyone in my class loves pencil toppers.

Here's my pencil topper top ten:

10. My bird on a spring
(I like the way it wobbles)

9. Emily's cute cat
(nothing special but I like its face)

8. My cute cat
(super curly tail)

7. Bella's chips
(because chips!)

6. Emily's apple tree →
(pencil is an actual twig!)

5. Chloe's moon rubber
(smells like bubblegum) →

4. Emily's cupcake →
(makes me hungry just looking at it)

3. Mustafa's windmill →
(it works... nuff said)

2. Chloe's pipecleaner spider
(made by me)
↖ ...only 7 legs but
it's the thought that counts !!

1st

Top Spot

My felt cloud
(made by Chloe) ↘

↖ actually good

Oh, and another thing about Emily:

I can't stand her.

And yeah yeah, I know that doesn't make me sound very nice. But I am nice, so maybe I don't mean *can't stand*. It's probably more an **extreme, ultra version** of dislike. And it's not just me. Chloe **ultra**-dislikes Emily too.

It's not because of the pencil toppers. And it's not because she's good at everything. It's because she lets you know she's good at everything. And then she lets you know you're not.

Anyway, *perfect* Emily wasn't letting me look at her work. She was doing that wall-of-arms thing and giving me sly-eye.

She's hiding it. You really don't know? Treja? Tresha? Tresher?

Nope. Don't know. Something to tell you.

Tretcha? Trejur?

Stop writing crazy words.
I have BIG NEWS!!!!!

???

Leaving Dungfields. Going to Lady Juniper's.

13

"What?!" I said.

Suddenly everyone was staring. It was like being in a room full of meerkats, all leaning in and super-alert.

Chloe shook her head, all frantic. She reminded me of a wet dog trying to shake off the drips.

I knew she wanted me to be quiet and I knew everyone was listening but I didn't even care.

"What???!!!" I said again.

And then there was a shadow on our table and I had a horrible feeling Mr Stilton was standing behind me. Which he was.

"I assume there's a reason you're disturbing the whole class?" he said.

"Yes," I said. **"Chloe is leaving Dungfields,"** I said. **"And Chloe is the only good thing about Dungfields,"** I said. **"And Dungfields will be rubbish without Chloe,"** I said. **"And I don't want to be in your rubbish class any more, either,"** I said.

(OK, I didn't actually say any of that stuff. I wanted to, but I didn't.)

Instead I just went quiet and huffy (which was probably not very clever either).

"Well, Molly?" said Mr Stilton. "Why were you shouting?"

"I can't spell something," I mumbled.

"Not good enough," he said. Then he sighed through his nose, and went and got a big tatty book from his desk.

He plonked it in front of me.

"It's called a **dictionary**," he said.

"Use it."

And then he wrote my name under the thundercloud.

I glared at the dictionary.

"Are you angry with me?" whispered Chloe.

I ignored her.

Was I angry with Chloe? No! Well maybe.
But mostly I was sad. Not just sad sad, but
shocked-sad – which is the worst kind of sad.
Shocked-sad hits you like a bucket of cold slime,
like, **SPLAT,** and suddenly your whole
life is drenched in gloom.

That's how bad I felt.

Anyway, I flicked through the dictionary but
my eyes were **BLURRING** (with all the

shocked-sad) so I couldn't see much. And then the big tatty book kind of broke into two bits. And one half fell on the floor. And then Mr Stilton said my name like I'd done it on purpose, which I really hadn't. It was just old.

"It was an accident," I said.

"Pick it up!" he said.

And that's when things got strange.

I bent down to get the dictionary and there was something else lying next to it. At first I thought one of the pages had come out, so I reached for it. But it wasn't a dictionary page. It was a scrap of notepaper with something drawn on it. A **scribbly, doodly** little witch.

She looked friendly and smiley and I wanted her to be real.

Which is **probably** why I sneaked my rainbow scissors from my pencil case. And it's **probably** why, when no one was looking,

I quickly cut her out. And it's **definitely** why

I thought something super-embarrassing as I

slipped her into the pencil pot.

is what I thought.

And then I forgot about her

because, let's face it, she wasn't real.

She wasn't.

And then, somehow,

she was.

CHAPTER TWO

At first, I didn't have a clue. It's not like I saw her climb out of the pencil pot or anything.

I was busy looking at the half of the dictionary with the letter "t" in it. I was looking up **trejure** and **tresher** and **tredger**. And honestly, I looked and looked and it took forever because the right spelling just wasn't in there.

So *that* was annoying.

And then something pinged off my head.

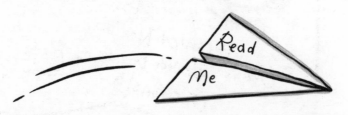

I unfolded the paper aeroplane.

Dear Molly,
Your sads has awokens me!
Is you is sads because you is stuck?
You is been chewing pencil for long
times. Yummy yes?
Sharpenings is best. I wants them
brekins, lunch and dins.
Soooooo..... gooooo...d!
Anyways, I is done super helpings!
I is done your writings! If you is
thinking hoorah and hooray, writes
YIPPEEEEEES! (And crumples your
letterings into penpot.)
Yours waitings,
Veronica Noates
P.S. You is alloweds to calls me Notes.
(For funs!)

First of all I thought someone was pranking. I couldn't work out who'd thrown it though. (Let's face it, everyone looks suspicious when you've been poked in the head with a paper aeroplane.)

So I wrote a note and stuck it in the pen pot. It went like this:

Who is this?

And why are you chucking planes at my head? I mean, OW!!

And then another plane poked me — in the
shoulder this time.

Read
me too

Dear Molly,

I is Notes! Notes is me!

Bestest wishes,

from Notes

P.S. Next times I is
leaving my letterings in
pen pot too.

Sorry for hurts!

This was getting silly. So I wrote to Chloe.

And then I wrote to Emily.

Emily, was that you?

Dear Molly,

Some of us are trying to plan our pirate stories. Please don't bother me again.

Emily

Hmm. So is that a yes or a no? Because if it's a yes, you're not funny.

Go away!

I started looking round the room again in case someone was looking and laughing. Because then I'd know they did it.

But instead I saw MR STILTON.

And he **definitely** wasn't laughing.

"Molly, can I see you?" said Mr Stilton (and in my head I was thinking, you're looking right at me, but I didn't say it).

I got up and I went to his desk. I thought
he was going to start grumbling at me for not
working. But he waved a bit of paper in my face
and he said,

"Is this a joke?"

And I said, "Wha—?!"

Then I looked at the paper. I looked at the scribbly, wriggly writing. And there it was. My name.

The Cursings of
Bony Parrot
by Molly Mills

(full story becouse plannings is boring!)

Once there is being a bony parrot and he is bony and he squaaaawks! And oh no says the pirates. And they also says stay awgy bony parrot! Too squawksome loud!

But bony parrot has old sea magics. and bony parrot squawks cursings.

P.T.O.

No more gold for mean grumpling pirates!

We is busting with sorries says ugly toothless and stinky tatter-clothes is crying and wobbly fur-face is pleading......

What is we to do ?!?!

Gives me chompy nuts and captain's hat he say and they say okey pokey.

And bony parrot is King Captain parrot.
(THE END)

My brain had pretty much stopped working by this point. All I could think was *"what the huh?!"* and *"what in the wah?!?"* ... What was going on??

"It's your own time you've wasted," said Mr Stilton. "You can stay in at break and do what I asked you to do."

"But I didn't write that!" I said.

And he said, **"So where's your work then?"**

And as soon as he said that I was stuck. Because I didn't actually have any work, and I couldn't exactly show him all the notes I'd been

writing, could I?! I couldn't say, "Ha! Look! Proof!
I was far too busy to write that silly story plan."
(Even though I really, really wanted to.)

So I just slunk back to my table, in a massive
(but totally not my fault) sulk.

I put it in the pen pot and waited.

And when I looked

again,

I found

this inside:

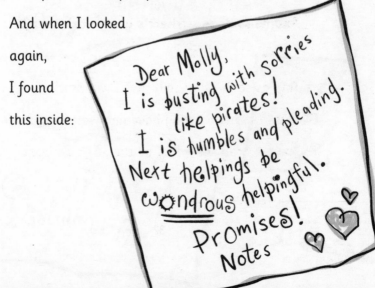

OK, now you're freaking me out. Been watching pen pot. No one's gone near it. How are you doing this? You a ghost?
Molly

Oh Molly, Notes is not ghosties! Ghosties is mostlies scallyweasles and boogerheads.
Notes is witchy.
Notes is secret scribble witchy.
Only friendlings can see.
Wants to see?
Notes
x

I want to see.

And we is friendlings?

Yes, fine.

Thing is, I still kind of thought it was a prank.

So, I wasn't ready for what happened next.

I wasn't ready for a paper witch **(my paper witch!!)** to climb out of the pen pot.

And I wasn't ready for her to stand there waving at me.

And I may have *squeaked* a bit.

Just a little teeny bit.

OK, it wasn't a bit, it was a lot. I couldn't help it. Inside I was screaming like

WAHHHHH??!!!

But I tried to keep it in, and this squeaking sound came out instead.

And then Mr Stilton said, "What was that?!" And Dylan B. said he'd heard a mouse. And Ruby D. said it wasn't a mouse, it was a rat. And she said that she saw it, which she totally didn't because it was me. The whole time, Chloe was looking at me trying to work out what I was doing. And Emily was frowning like I was so childish when she was so grown-up which was so not true.

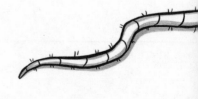

Because they couldn't see the little scribble witch standing there, tiny finger on her teeny, tiny lips.

CHAPTER THREE

Emily **tutted** and turned her back on me
**(which was actually perfect because I needed
to write to Notes)**. And even though Chloe
was still watching me, confused, I made myself
pick up a pen and start writing, pretending like
nothing had happened. I hoped Chloe would
think I was writing my pirate plan.

Dear Notes,
   I'm feeling a bit ~~flabagastid~~
~~flabbygastid~~ shocked. I never saw a tiny
person before. Plus you're all squiggly
and doodly. I need a moment to think
about this.
   Molly

I didn't need to put the note in the pen pot because Notes was already sitting there reading it.

And while this was going on, Mr Stilton was ranting and saying stuff like, "There are no rats in this classroom!"

Which was funny really. Because Stilton is a kind of cheese, right? And if I was a rat I would so visit Mr Cheese. I'd be like:

"Huh? A man made of cheese? Let's go!"

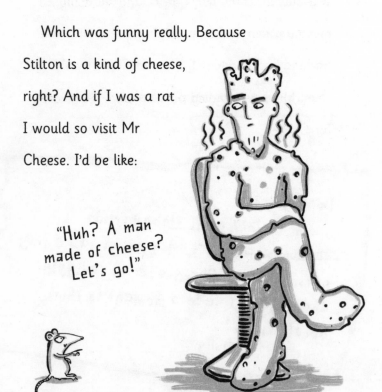

And normally stuff like that would make me laugh out loud. But I was a bit **FREAKED OUT** by my new witchy friendling. And still a bit shocked-sad about Chloe. So I didn't laugh.

(But I didn't squeak either which is good.)

Anyway, then it was break and suddenly no one cared about rats.

All the kids bundled out the room. All except for Chloe.

"You all right?" she said.

I wasn't all right.

"Not really," I said.

A lot was happening all at once. Chloe was leaving, Notes had appeared out of nowhere. Nothing made sense any more.

Chloe looked at me then at the floor then at me again.

She was being sheepish. That's what my nan calls it. Sheepish is like a mix of awkward and embarrassed and it's a stupid word because it's got nothing to do with sheep.

Chloe (sheepish)

Sheep (not sheepish)

But that's what she was being. So I kind of had a clue that she was about to say something even worse.

"Tomorrow's my last day," she said.

I had no idea it would be that bad.

"Tomorrow's your last day??!"
I said.

"I know it's a bit sudden ..." she said.

"a bit sudden??!" I said.

"Stop copying what I'm saying," she said.

"Stop copying what you're saying?!" I said.

And maybe I was very slightly *too* shouty because then Mr Stilton came over. He told Chloe to go outside. And he said I had to take my work to the hall with the other no-playtime kids.

The whole time this was going on, the little witch was there, watching, listening. And when Mr Cheesy said that thing about taking my work to the hall, she stuck her head into the pen pot.

She pulled out the tattiest, most chewed-up pencil, and she clicked her fingers.

And **vooosh!** Up went the pencil.

It did this hovering thing, like a broomstick, and she just hopped right on.

Then she took off on it. Of course she did. I shouldn't have been surprised. Of course the witch from my pencil case had a flying pencil. Of course the **craziness** would just keep getting crazier.

I could see her from the corner of my eye, flying right alongside my left ear as I walked down the corridor.

"What are you doing?!" I whispered.

She smiled but just kept flying.

"You can't come too!" I said.

She stopped flying. She stopped smiling too.

"I do want you to come," I said, turning back to her. I had no idea if I meant it. "But I won't be able to concentrate if you're there. And I really, *really* need to write my pirate story plan

46

so I don't get in more trouble."

She smiled again.

"OK," I said. "So you'll go back to the pen pot
and wait for me?"

She shook her head.

"So you *won't* go back to class?"

She grinned and nodded.

"Perfect," I mumbled.

↖ And just to be clear, it really wasn't.

Then off we went (again).

Soon we were going through the hall's big double doors. And there was Mrs Banton with her **NO-PLAYTIME LIST**, and her cranky frown.

My heart was **thunking**, my sweaty fingers gripped my story plan.

Now maybe you're reading this and you're thinking so what? Missing playtime is no big deal. But for me it's a humungous deal. I have literally never missed a playtime (except this one) in my whole entire life.

It's not that I'm Miss Goody McGoody-Knickers or anything.

MISS GOODY MC GOODY KNICKERS

NOT ME!

I'm not saying that. I **do** get in trouble. But I'm normally good at getting in just the right amount of trouble. And this was the wrong amount.

So I was **extremely** embarrassed when Mrs Banton saw me there. And **extra-extremely** embarrassed when the other no-playtime kids started looking.

There were maybe ten of them, sitting on the floor. Some looked **GROUCHY**, some looked **BORED**, some just picked their noses and looked out of the window.

I joined them.

The witch landed beside me on the floor.
She climbed off her pencil and sat like me, legs
crossed. And she winked.

The wink worried me. Winking is what you do when you've got a **secret plan.** It's what you do when you're up to something.

And in my head I was thinking this:

Stay calm. It'll be OK. As long as she doesn't try to help again. But nah – she wouldn't. Not after last time.

I probably should have known better.

CHAPTER FOUR

She'd scribbled the message on the floor beside me before I could stop her.

"No helpings!" I hissed. "And no writing on the floor!"

Well, straight away, she started writing again. But this time I'm talking crazy fast writing. Magic fast. So fast I could hardly see her. There was just this mad mess of swirling whirling scribbles, and then there it was ...

Sorry abouts writings but
Notes loves notes! (Don't worry though.)
No one can see Notes' notes unless
Notes wants notes seen. Understands?
Even Notes' pencil is been made
invisibles!
(such wondrous magics!)
I probble should tell friendling
Molly PLEASE no tellings!
friendling Molly must not tell
Chloe or Emily or grouchbag
Mr Teachings or cross-face
teacher in hall.
Molly must keep secret.
Zip!

I must have looked weird reading all that, staring at the floor with my mouth open. And I wanted to know why ... *why did Notes have to be a secret?* And I would've asked her but I couldn't.

Because Benji Staples had noticed me being peculiar and he was whispering to Harry Davis. And then Harry Davis whispered something to Jess Pritty. And then everyone was elbowing everyone, and pointing and staring.

So then Mrs Banton started giving me **THE LOOK.** You know – the *whatever you're doing stop it now* look? And did you ever notice how hard it is to act innocent when you're getting that look?

Anyway, I pretended I was really thinking hard. Really doing some Proper Careful Thinking about my pirate story plan.

Which I so wasn't.
This is what I was really thinking:

There's a witch sitting next to me...

Chloe's leaving...

Choe can't leave...

Why's Chloe leaving?

So I couldn't concentrate on my pirate story plan. Not with all that going on in my head.

What I needed was a moment. Just one quiet moment to figure out what the **fruiting flapjacks** was happening.

What I didn't need was Harry lobbing a scrunched-up piece of paper at me with this on it.

And what I really didn't need was what happened next.

You see, Notes saw it. She saw it and she looked at Harry, and then she started changing.

She went from this

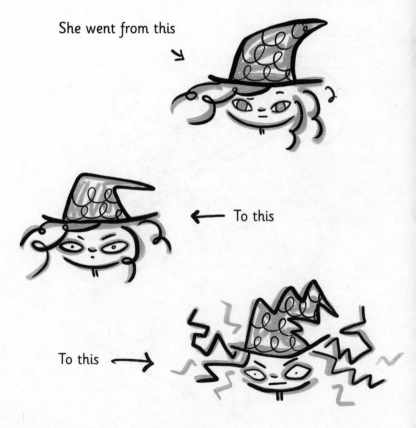

To this

To this ——→

And then she grabbed the drawing and she grabbed my pencil. Not her pencil – the magic one, the one only I could see. *My* pencil.

Which meant that whatever she was up to, it wasn't secret.

"What are you doing?!" I whispered.

She wasn't listening.

She flipped over Harry's drawing and she scribbled something on the back.

And then she threw it.

SCORE!

It hit Harry right on the nose. (Which was

half-IMPRESSIVE,
half-YIKES!)

Notes grinned at me, all happy and doodly again.

And I know she was only trying to help, but this was a bad time to be throwing paper balls at **annoying** boys.

"Molly Mills!" said Mrs Banton.

"It wasn't me, Miss!" I said (which was the worst thing to say, I know, I know).

"Give me that," she said to Harry.
"Oh, Molly!"

She held up the paper:

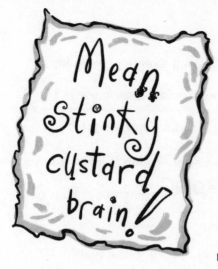
Mean Stinky custard brain!

"I didn't do it! And look – look on the back. It's me! I mean, it's not *me*. My eyes don't do that, and my tongue doesn't loll out like that, and to be honest the hair's a bit neater than mine, 'cos I forgot to brush it this morning. But it's *meant* to be me! Look!"

"And your point, Molly?" asked Mrs Banton.

And she gave me **THE LOOK** again, that just instantly makes you feel guilty, even when you're not.

"My – my point?" What even *was* my point? "My point is ... w-why would I draw myself? I wouldn't, that's why. I mean – not why. I mean, how. No, not how." This whole speech was going **HORRIBLY WRONG.**

"That's quite enough, Molly. I saw you writing, and you've not been doing your class work. So clearly you wrote this."

"But ..." But what could I say? **Nothing.**

"Well, as you like writing notes so much, you can write one to Mr Stilton. You can explain why you've wasted your time instead of doing your work."

Which made no sense at all if you think about it.

I didn't argue. You don't push your luck with
Mrs Banton.

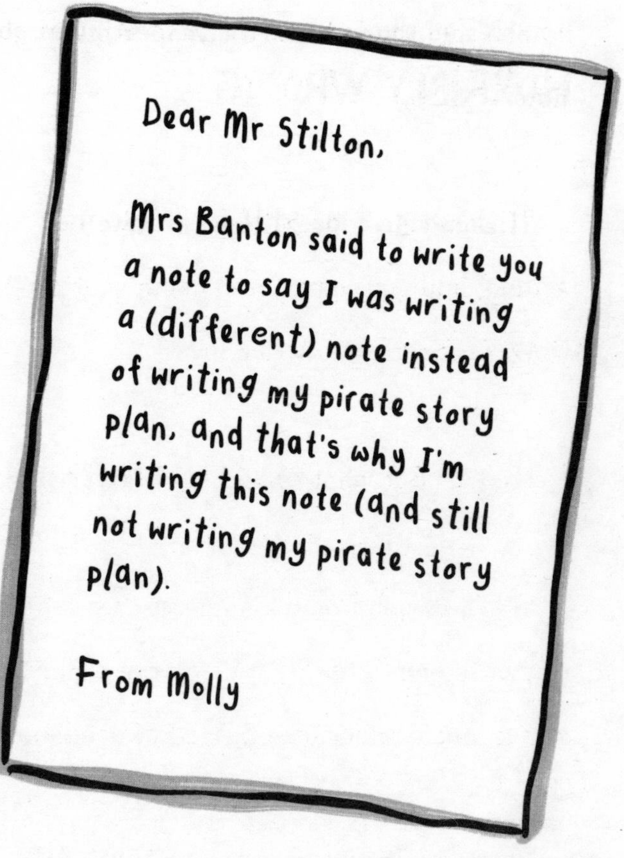

Dear Mr Stilton,

Mrs Banton said to write you
a note to say I was writing
a (different) note instead
of writing my pirate story
plan, and that's why I'm
writing this note (and still
not writing my pirate story
plan).

From Molly

Mrs Banton sent me back to class after that, because playtime was finished.

She said she'd check I'd given Mr Stilton the note.

(I didn't give Mr Stilton the note.)

CHAPTER FIVE

I know, I know. I should have just handed it over, straight away. I should have and I didn't.

But he was busy sorting maths questions and everyone was chatting and I wanted to speak to Chloe. And OK, OK, I was terrified.

So the note for Mr Stilton had to wait a bit. *Maybe he'd just forget about it,* I thought.

Anyway, I went straight over to Chloe and I was about to say something about how changing schools was a **crazy** idea. But I didn't get a chance because she spoke first.

"Here," she said.

She gave me a note.

"Huh?" I said. "What's this?"

"It's about me leaving. I wanted to explain face to face but—"

She sighed, "But then I saw how weird you got before break, copying everything I said."

"Copying everything you said?"

Chloe rolled her eyes. "Really?! Again?"

"Sorry. I'm not doing it on purpose."

"So I changed my mind," she said. "I've
written you a letter instead."

Dear Molly,

So yeah, I'm leaving Dungfields.
Tomorrow is my last day. I'm
starting Lady Juniper's on
Wednesday and I'm excited about
it. But I'm also REEEEEEALLY going to
miss you. We can still do stuff out
of school. Sleepovers and stuff. And
you'll always be my best friend.
Hope you understand.

From Chloe x

I looked up at Chloe, and she smiled, and she raised her eyebrows in a questioning kind of way. Like maybe I'd be OK with this now that she'd written it down with extra Es for "reeeeeeally". Oh, so she'd miss me, huh?!? If she was going to miss me so much then why was she going?

How was she not upset about it? I was upset.

I was a mess! And I had to look away because I was going to start crying.

'It's not that bad,' Chloe said, and that just made me feel even worse. Maybe it was no big deal to her that we'd been best friends ever since nursery. Ever since that day I got my head stuck in that gate and she put her head through the bars too, to show me how easy it was to get out. Which it wasn't, of course, and then we were both stuck and bawling our eyes out until the fire brigade came and rescued us.

And what about when she moved house and she was so scared of her big **SHADOWY** bedroom, and I gave her my unicorn nightlight with the wonky horn? Didn't that mean **anything** to her?

Or that time when I had an earwig in my hair and everyone screamed (including me) but she knocked it off!

That stuff was important to me! Wasn't it important to her?

"Are you OK?" she said.

I didn't say anything.

"Molly?" she said.

And then Mr Stilton coughed, and he pointed at the board with his metre stick.

I sat down in my seat, and then gasped. I'd forgotten all about Notes while this was going on.

She was sitting on the edge of the pen pot,

and had clearly been watching and listening

to me and Chloe. When everyone else turned

to look at the board, Notes dragged her magic

pencil up close and wrote on the table.

Is Molly sads?
Is Molly needs more helpings?

I shook my head.

Is it yOu is needs Cross Notes
with zig-zag hair? Notes does
cross helpings for Molly?

"*No!*" I whispered. I didn't want to be rude, but her helpings weren't actually helping.

"What was that, Molly?" said Mr Stilton.

"Nothing," I said. I wiped my eyes.

"Nothing! That's **excellent**, Molly. Quite right. The answer is zero. Come up here and show us how you did it," he said.

And before you start thinking he was being nice to me, think again. Because I'm almost one hundred per cent sure he knew I meant nothing. I mean actual nothing. Not zero. And here he was, making me do a *stand-up-in-front-of-everyone* maths performance.

I'm OK at maths, don't get me wrong. But not with people staring at me.

Anyhow, I got up and went to the front and picked up a white board marker.

I have a cake.
My dog eats $\frac{3}{6}$
my cat eats $\frac{1}{4}$
and $\frac{2}{8}$ falls on the floor.
What do I have left?

It wasn't so hard. Problem was, my brain had turned to **mush** from all the sadness and weird stuff that had happened today. So for a while I just stood there looking at the silly question. I could feel everyone's eyes on me, like laser dots.

And my cheeks started **burning** from all the

lasering, and Mr Stilton tapped his foot, but I

still didn't know what to do.

Right when I thought I was at maximum

embarrassment, it got worse. Notes decided to

help. Again.

She swooped in front of me. Then, still sitting

on her magic pencil, she wrote on the board.

Is cake chocolate cake? Dog can't eats chocolate.
Sick dog if eats chocolate cake. Cats is sames.
Cats hates all cake. Unless is meat cake?
Happy cats is for meaty cake.
Yums and meeeows! Cake on floor is still goods.
So answer is $\frac{2}{8}$?

I looked at the class. They looked at me. They didn't look like they could see what I could see.

"Molly?" said Mr Stilton. "Can we see your working out, please?"

I couldn't think straight.

"W-what kind of cake is it?" I said.

He raised an eyebrow. "Why? It doesn't matter."

"Dogs and cats can't eat chocolate. It's really bad for them. If it's a chocolate cake then—"

"It's not. It's a vanilla sponge. Just answer the question, Molly."

I looked at the numbers, $\frac{3}{6}$ ... $\frac{1}{4}$ ... $\frac{2}{8}$ ... But I couldn't remember what I was supposed to do with them. Divide the bottom bit? Times the top bit??

÷ ? ✗ ? !

And everyone was waiting, staring, so I had to say something.

"What's wrong with the bit on the floor? You could still eat it. Just pick it up quick and blow on it."

"Molly, are you trying to tell me you can't show us your working?" he said.

It wasn't fair! I could do it. Normally, I really could have.

But I was too nervous (about getting it wrong) and embarrassed (about saying all that cake stuff) and distracted (by Notes) and miserable (about Chloe).

How could anyone feel all that stuff all at once AND do maths?!

But then something happened.

birthday meaty sponge with the sprinkles

tasty floor cake

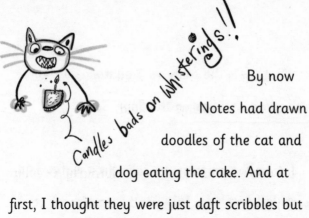

Candles bads on Whisterings!!

By now
Notes had drawn
doodles of the cat and
dog eating the cake. And at
first, I thought they were just daft scribbles but
they weren't! Not if you looked properly. They
made sense!

"The dog's got half the cake," I said.

"Go on," said Mr Stilton.

"And the cat's got ... a-a quarter?" I said.

"Yes," he said. "Keep going."

"And $\frac{2}{8}$ is the same as a quarter ... I think ...
so that means $\frac{1}{4}$ is on the floor. So ..."

I drew the parts of the cake (like Notes had
done, but less squiggly) and I stood back to
admire my work. Finally it made sense!

"Marvellous, Molly. Well done," he said.
And for a moment, a teeny tiny moment, I was
fooled.

He's being kind, I thought. Maybe he isn't so bad, I thought. Gah! How wrong was I!?

Because then Mr Stilton said this: "I think you should try the harder questions today, Molly, don't you?"

And I said, "No, I don't."

But he said, "Yes, you do."

And I said, "Oh."

And I could have kicked myself.

Because nothing had changed. He was still moody Mr Cheese.

CHAPTER SIX

There's not much to say about the rest of Maths.
I did all the work (take that, Mr Stilton) but I
didn't talk to Chloe again. Not even with notes.
And talking of notes, I didn't talk to actual Notes
either. Although I did put a little scrap of paper
in the pen pot:

Thanks for your
helpings. It did
actually, you know,
help. Molly x

She used it as a blanket and went to sleep.
Guess she'd had a busy morning.

Z Z Z Z Z Z Z Z Z

Getting back to the Chloe thing though – I wasn't ignoring her. I bet she thought I was. But I really wasn't. It's just that

1. I was thinking about the maths,

and

2. I didn't know what to say to her.

What do you say to someone you thought was your best friend for years and years when actually they don't care about you at all? Not a lot, is what you say. And so, by the time it was lunch, I'd done a whole load of maths in a whole load of **silence.** Which is really not like me.

OK, I did talk a tiny bit. To Emily, who was

also doing the hard questions.

She was doing the arm-wall thing again, and I said, "I'm not copying you, you know! You don't have to sit like that."

And she said, "Sure," but in a snotty voice.

And I said, "I'm not. I'm almost finished. Look."

So she did look, and at first she was all,
"You can't just write any old thing, you know. It
actually has to make sense."

But then she looked a bit more and she
must have seen it did make sense, because she
changed some of her answers.

So then it was me doing the arm-wall thing.

Mr Stilton was doing this weird GHOSTLY walk he does when he wants to snoop on how well you're doing. And when he got to me he mumbled "Huh!" like he was still surprised that I actually had a brain. Then he said something odd.

He said, "Thanks for your note, Molly. I'll read it when I get a moment."

↖ Which was a VERY strange thing to say, because the note to Mr Stilton was hidden in my pencil case.

A teeny worry fluttered in my chest. What if this had something to do with Notes? What if she had been doing more of her secret "helpings"?

Mr Stilton was still standing behind me,

waiting for me to say something. So I just said

"uh-huh"

like I knew what he was talking about, and

hoped that'd be the last of it.

(It really, really wasn't, but I'll get to that later.)

Lunchtime came around and Chloe asked if

I wanted to sit on the outside benches to have

our packed lunches. But we hadn't spoken for the

whole of maths, so it suddenly felt a bit weird

speaking now.

So I just kind of shrugged and said, "Do what

you want."

And she said, "What?"

And I said, "Do what you want."

And she said, "Is this about the letter?"

And I didn't reply.

So she said, "Fine! Be like that!" and she went off to sit with Ruby and Sita who are in the year above.

And yeah – O𝕂 – it was about the letter, and – 𝕟O – I probably shouldn't have said "do what you want". But I was upset and sometimes when I'm upset I say **GRUMPY** stuff that I feel bad about later.

And this time, later was straight away. I almost followed her and said sorry. Almost. But I was still upset – that hadn't changed – though now I was upset and sorry at the same time.

So it was complicated.

Anyway, in the end I had to sit outside because it was pizza day and the canteen was packed, so that was a bit rubbish.

I sat at one end of the long picnic bench, and Chloe, Ruby and Sita sat at the other end. A bunch of kids sat between us but it was still super-awkward. I almost wished Notes would appear.

Then I wouldn't feel so all on my own. And for a mini moment I thought maybe I saw something out the corner of my eye. Something little and doodly zooming past.

But when I looked, there were definitely no scribble witches around to keep me company.

I sighed and opened my lunchbox. Disaster. My yoghurt had leaked. Normally I wouldn't get embarrassed by leaky yoghurt. Normally I would get cranky and clean it off and make a big thing about it because it's so annoying. But this time it was embarrassing. Because Chloe was half watching me. Watching and thinking how much I deserved to have my lunch covered in yoghurt. I knew that's what she would be thinking.

I kept the lid of my lunchbox sticking up so she wouldn't be able to see. And I looked at the damage.

Everything was pink.

Even Mum's note was so smudged I couldn't make it out.

I should probably explain about Mum's notes.

She always puts a note in my lunch.

Just saying stuff like ...

Or ...

Or ...

Or sometimes she'd do a little doodle. Like ...

Or ...

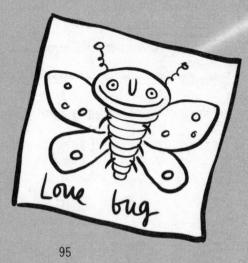

Today's doodle looked like it had started its life as a smiley face, but now it looked like...

You make me...

So I put it to one side and poked at my food.

My apple was totally gooped. I could have saved it but that would have been messy. Same with my bag of salty popcorn. At least my sandwich is safe, I thought. Safely wrapped in tin foil. My favourite – cheese, cucumber, sweetcorn and tomato sauce sandwich. So, even though the foil was icky with strawberry yoghurt, I did still want to eat it.

Carefully, carefully, I pinched the corners. Gently, gently, I peeled back the foil. And all my hopes died a yoghurty death. There was a tear in the foil. A tear! Which meant yoghurt had leaked in. Which meant half of my best-ever sandwich was wet and GROSS.

Which meant I was now totally, absolutely

100% fed up.

This had to be my absolute number one worst lunch disaster ever (and that's saying something, I've had a few).

Top ten lunch disasters:

10. The time Mum forgot to put a spoon in and I had to eat a _whole_ chocolate mousse with my thumb. (Actually not that bad.)

9. The time I dropped my cereal bar and Chloe stepped on it. I still ate it, obviously, because it was in the packet.

8. The time my bottle lid was screwed so tight that even Mrs Guthman (who has superhero-sized muscles) couldn't open it.

7. The time my orange squash leaked all over my reading record.

READING RECORD

6. The time Harry Davis nicked my crisps and said he didn't (and I couldn't prove it, but he never normally has salt and vinegar corn puffs and I _ALWAYS_ do.)

5. The time Mum gave me celery. **Celery!!**

← !?!

4. The time Dad made me a fruit salad (which I normally love) but everything somehow tasted of onion.

← chewy disappointment

3. The time I thought I had chocolate chip cookies but they turned out to be raisin cookies instead.

2. The time I forgot my lunchbox altogether and had to have school dinners.
Cauliflower-cheese.
I can't even talk about it, it's too upsetting.

1. The yoghurt thing. Gah!

It was at this point I felt a burny feeling behind my eyes. And I knew I was going to start crying. Not just over the yoghurt. Obviously not.

It was everything.

It was all just too much.

0

0

0

CHAPTER SEVEN

I really, really, really didn't want to cry in front of Chloe (and Ruby and Sita). So I clicked my lunchbox lid shut and I left.

I sort of hoped Chloe would follow me to see if I was OK.

She didn't.

Fine. I was better off on my own anyway.
    (That's what I told myself, but it's not true.)

I decided I'd go to the Secret Spot. The Secret

Spot is at the far end of the field and it's not actually secret, but at least you can be on your own there if you want.

See, the Secret Spot is this big bush you can climb inside. But no one really does except me and Chloe.

So I went past the footballers, past the skipping-ropers, past the hula-hoopers, right across the field to the overgrown bit at the bottom.

I stood there, in front of the Secret Spot, still kind of thinking Chloe might come.

So when someone tapped me on the shoulder
I spun round.

"Chloe?" I said.

But it wasn't Chloe at all. In fact the pokey
thing hadn't been a finger but a pencil
(the blunt end thankfully).

"Notes!" I said. "It's you!"

She grinned and nodded.

"Quick! In here," I said, climbing into the
Secret Spot. "Wait. What are you doing to those
leaves?"

Notes had grabbed a big bunch of leaves from
the bush on her way in.

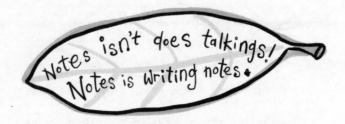

"But this is the Secret Spot!" I said. "You can
just talk. No one will hear."

"You can't talk?"

Notes shrugged.

Notes likes notes betters.

"Oh. How did you even know where to find me?" I said.

Notes dids secret follows.

Huh. OK. Bit creepy but kind of handy. I had so many important questions to ask her. Starting with, "Why do I have to keep you secret?"

105

Notes grabbed another leaf and whizzed into super-speedy scribble-write mode.

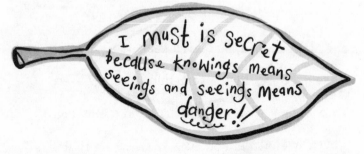

I must is secret because knowings means seeings and seeings means danger!!

She looked me in the eye, **DEAD SERIOUS.** Then she grabbed my hand and started writing on it!

Has you is seens what peoples does with scribbly doodles on papery scrappings?! Peoples does scrumplings and scrimplings and (baddliest of bads) rippings!!!

106

Fair point. She didn't want to end up in the
bin.

"Don't worry, Notes. I'll keep your secret,"
I said. "Um ... there's something else I've been
wondering ... Hope you don't mind me asking,
but ... who drew you?"

Good askings!
I is been drawn looong
time ago by sad child.

I is been waiting
so long to be founds.

And then wondrous
Molly was sads and
cuts me out.

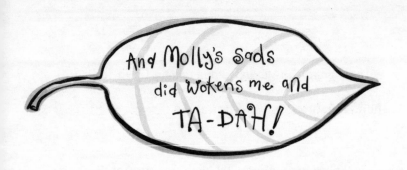

And Molly's sads
did wokens me and
TA-DAH!

I suddenly felt bad. "You're kind of all alone,
aren't you?"

Here I was, moping about Chloe, when Notes
had no one. NO ONE. I haven't met many other
little scribble witches zipping around the planet.

Notes not alones!
Notes has friendling
Molly!

"Well, yeah, but other than me, I mean."
Because let's face it, I'd been a rubbish friend to
Notes so far.

Notes shrugged and smiled, and sort of hugged my thumb, so I got a MAJOR case of the guilts.

"I'll be a good friend from now on," I said, and I really meant it.

Of course!
We is already best friendlings!

She grinned up at me and I grinned back, and then I remembered my other best friend. The human one. The one who was leaving me.

It was my turn to shrug.

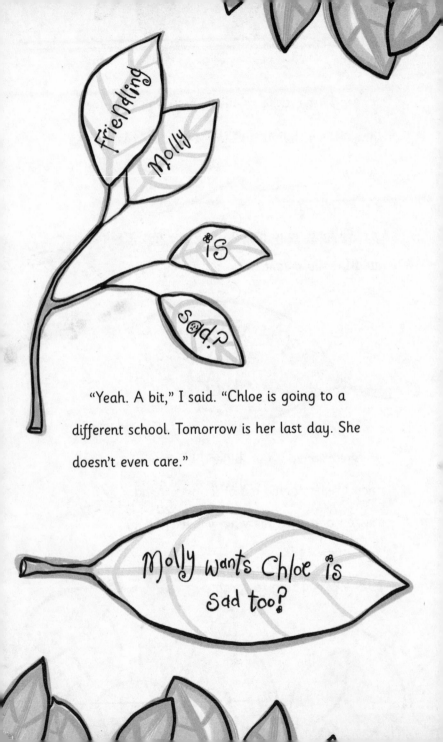

Friendling Molly is sad?

"Yeah. A bit," I said. "Chloe is going to a different school. Tomorrow is her last day. She doesn't even care."

Molly wants Chloe is sad too?

Did I want that? Maybe I did. Was that bad?

"No," I said, but wasn't quite sure if I meant it.

Molly wants Chloe is missing Molly as equals as Molly is missing Chloe?

I had to read that three times before I got

what she meant. But yeah, clever Notes. That's

what I wanted. I wanted to know Chloe would

miss me as much as I'd miss her.

(Which, by the way, was loads.)

"I guess so," I said.

The little witch nodded.

Just then, my tummy rumbled. It was a loud rumble. A cross between hungry (because I still was) and stressy (because, well, you know why).

But when Notes heard it, she stood up extra straight. And she poked her finger in the air like she'd remembered something. Then she lifted up her hat, pulled something out, and offered it to me.

"Pencil sharpenings?" I said. "Why have you got sharpenings under your hat?"

But then I remembered what she'd said about eating them for brekins, lunch and dins.

"Oh! That's kind but no thanks. People don't eat sharpenings."

She shrugged, plopped down on her pencil and started eating. And that's how she stayed for a very long time. I guess those sharpenings are quite chewy.

So Notes sat there eating, and I sat there hoping Chloe would come. She didn't. Eventually the bell went and it was time to go in.

"I can carry you if you like," I said. "Easier than flying."

But Notes wanted to fly on her pencil (it did look more fun). So she rode alongside my left ear.

When we got to class, Chloe was already there. She was sitting at our table, chatting. It was like nothing had happened, except she was talking to Emily (which she NEVER normally does). And when I walked in, they both looked at me, and Chloe looked away again, but Emily kept staring and frowning and shaking her head.

So then I knew Chloe had been talking about me and maybe said something horrible.

I sat down in between them and pretended I wasn't interested. It felt really rubbishy though. Like I was the odd one out, when usually it's Emily.

Being the odd one out stank.

CHAPTER EIGHT

I played with the zip of my pencil case, trying really hard to send out *I-don't-care* vibes. But of course I cared. I cared loads. I cared so much I started feeling guilty about all those times Emily was left out (even though she was annoying). Because now I knew it's really not much fun.

Not that I was alone of course. Notes was there, perched on the edge of my pencil case.

That made me feel a bit better. Knowing I had a friend. It helped me not to cry. If Notes wasn't there, I would have cried for **definite**.

But instead, when Mr Stilton called the register, I didn't mumble "here" like I was all upset. I just said it – "here!" – like I was fine.

It wasn't **all** bad. Monday afternoon we always do art **(which is my best lesson × 100 and always has been)**. I love art because you don't have to get it right. You just do it and see what happens. Plus you don't have to do it again if it all turns into **a big wet painty mess** that drips all over the carpet on the way to the bin **(but you do have to write a letter to the cleaner to say sorry)**.

Anyway, after register, Mr Stilton asked me to hand out the sketchbooks. And that was better than being the odd one out, so I did it extra slowly.

When I got back to the table there was no Chloe and there was no Emily.

Turns out Mr Stilton had sent them to borrow some sketching pencils from Mrs Banton.

So, I was going to sit down. But when I pulled out my chair, I saw something. Right there, on the seat, was a note.

First of all I thought Notes had written it.

My second guess would have been Chloe. But it

wasn't from either of them. It was from Emily.

Dear Molly,

I don't understand why you're
being mean to Chloe. Chloe thinks
you don't like her any more
because she's leaving. Did you even
bother to ask her why she's going?
I know you didn't. Sort it out.

Emily

Well, that was a bit rude. And also a bit

interesting.

Because why did she care if I sorted it out or not?

Anyway, I wasn't mean to Chloe. She was the one leaving. That was mean. Wasn't it?

But, I hadn't asked Chloe why. Emily was right about that.

Earlier, I was too upset to ask things like why. And I was muddled with pirate story plans and paper witches and stuff.

Now, it was a bit awkward. I didn't know if Chloe would even talk to me.

"What should I do, Notes?" I whispered.

Notes wrote across the table in her magic
pencil.

Tell Chloe what thinkings
and abouts sads and
missing Chloe.

Yeah, I thought (I was getting really good at
working out what she meant).

So I flipped over Emily's note and started
writing.

Chloe,
Sorry for being grumpy
earlier. I'm sad you're
going because I'll miss you
so much. Why do you have
to leave?

Molly x

I gave it to Chloe as soon as she got back to class (after she'd given out the pencils). And I watched her read it.

Then, super-quick, she grabbed a scrap of paper and started scribbling a new note.

Hi!
Thanks for saying sorry. Mum's been trying to get me into Lady Juniper's since we moved house. Dungfields takes sooooo long to walk to (I counted once except at 1564 steps I got muddled and had to stop). But Lady Juniper's is 87 steps from our house (I counted that too). So that's why.
Chloe x

Oh yeah. I suppose that makes sense.
Sorry. I just thought you didn't seem that
upset about it.

Molly x

This time she whispered, instead of writing.
Which is probably best, because there was loads
to say.

"I am upset and also not," she said. "I like
Lady Juniper's. There's a **swimming pool**
and there's a special hall with a **stage**
and **spotlights.** And some
of the kids sleep at the school,
although not me, because
I live **87 steps**
away. Plus I met my

 teacher and she's really smiley and she says there are only **13 kids** in the class and I'll be number **14** so that stops them being unlucky! But of course I'm sad about going too. I'm going to miss you **so much.**"

"Me too!!"

"You're going to miss yourself?"

"Hahaha."

"So can we hug now?"

So we hugged. Hurrah!

What a relief! Best friends again.

Notes did a spinny dance in celebration. Emily rolled her eyes and shook her head, but she was smiling a little bit.

But the thing is, while we were being best friends again, Mr Stilton had been busy too. He was reading a note on a little piece of paper, and whatever it said was now making him madder than mad.

"Molly!" he said, and everyone went quiet. Because he didn't say it like he wanted a chat, he said it like he wanted me to walk the plank.

And then he coughed, and he read the note

out loud:

Dear Mr Teachings,
   I is wanting to tell you that
I is so sorrying! Pirate writings was
bad writings! I promise fastest
and bestest pirate writings.
I promise focusing and good thinkings.
And most importance, I promise
wondrous listenings to all
Mr Teachings boringness for evers
and evers. Yours sorrying,
                           Molly

So that was the note Mr Stilton had

mentioned before lunch.

The class g̶a̶s̶p̶e̶d̶ all at once.

My mouth dropped open in total horror. Notes climbed on to her pencil and flew up to my face. She heaved my jaw shut and she pushed at the corners of my mouth, desperately trying to make me smile, but it wasn't happening. I wasn't angry with her, not really. She'd clearly written the note because she wanted to help **(again)**. But this was a nightmare.

"Another joke!?" said Mr Stilton. "How very ... creative of you."

A few kids laughed, nervously. I didn't dare, even though a tiny part of me thought it was hilarious.

"No, I'm not laughing either, Molly," said Mr Stilton. "You're playing the clown. There's nothing funny about clowns. Where is your pirate plan?" he said.

Gulp. Gulpety gulp.

Anyway, I'll give you the quick version of this bit of the story. Because it's not much fun.

Basically, I couldn't give him the story plan because there wasn't one. And I didn't get to do art, because the story plan was more important (to Mr Stilton, not to me).

So I sat in the quiet corner, next to the poster that says "FIVE WAYS TO CALM DOWN".

129

And I wrote my pirate story plan.

It wasn't my best writing ever, but at least it was done. Finished. The end.

It was about a bony parrot and a horrible curse and some greedy pirates. Because without the funny talk, Notes' story was actually all right.

Seemed like Notes was turning out to be pretty helpful after all.

Which was good.

Because I'd had an idea to make Chloe stay. And I couldn't do it alone.

CHAPTER NINE

I gave my story plan to Mr Stilton and he
mumbled something under his beard.

Then I sat back at my normal table.

Everyone else had been
drawing each other.

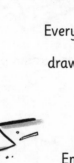

Chloe was doing
Emily's portrait
and Emily was
doing Chloe's
portrait, and they were still
finishing.

Notes was drawing too.
She was drawing one of
Emily's pencil toppers.
A cute but blobby-
looking cat.

I wrote
quickly on
a scrap of paper and
pushed it towards my witchy friend.

You OK? I've been
thinking about Chloe
leaving. Maybe we can
do something.

Notes is very OK, thank yous.
Notes likes doing cat pawtrait.
Molly likes Notes' doodlings.
And yes—Notes is been thinkings
too. Notes is thinking
wondrous plan!

Yeah - good drawing- nice ears. So what's
your plan? Are you thinking what I'm
thinking? I was thinking maybe Chloe could
be your friendling too.

I'd had this idea, you see. If Dungfields was

better than Lady Juniper's, maybe Chloe would

want to stay. Maybe Chloe would go on and on

and on and on at her mum.

And eventually her mum would say, **"Fine,
stay at Dungfields. I'll keep walking you all that
way to school and back every single day. Just**

PLEASE STOP GOING ON ABOUT IT!"

Although, making Dungfields better than Lady
Juniper's was tricky.

There was a lot of good stuff at Lady
Juniper's:

- **Swimming pool**
- **Special stage with spotlights**
- **Smiley teacher**

Dungfields had diddly. Less than diddly.
Dungfields had diddly squat. And in case you
don't know, diddly squat means

BIG FAT NOTHING.

Except now Dungfields did have something,
didn't it! It had a witch! A really cool little paper
witchy! Lady Juniper's didn't have one of those!

Notes was now scribbling on the table right in
front of me, all excited.

Notes is thinking exact sames!
Notes must be friendling of Chloe!
Notes thinks yes, absolutings
Yes!!!

Amazing! I could have hugged her! Except I'd probably have accidentally squished her. Plus to everyone else it would look like I was hugging myself. So I didn't. But I did whisper "thank you". And I really, really, really meant it.

So now the big question was: how to tell Chloe ...

Should I whisper it? Write it in a note? Should Notes write to her like she did to me? Probably. Possibly. What did Notes think?

How are we going to tell Chloe about you?

I writes it of course!

She disappeared into my pencil case, pulled a scrap of paper from my mini notepad, and she started writing.

Dear Chloe,
Surprise! There is a secrets in this room and TA-DAH! Secrets is ... me! Wants to know who is me? If yes, friendling Molly will tell you whats to do.
Byezees!
Notes

Notes started folding it into an aeroplane but I stopped her. She clapped her hands to her mouth, remembering **(maybe)** about "the hurts".

I pointed to Chloe's pencil case.

I love Chloe's pencil case. I've got one too and so has Emily. So have lots of kids in our class. But Chloe's is best of all.

Our pencil cases are where we keep our bits and bobs and fancy rubbers and rulers and sharpeners and pens and pencils and **(most important of all)** our pencil toppers.

Emily's pencil case is the biggest, of course.

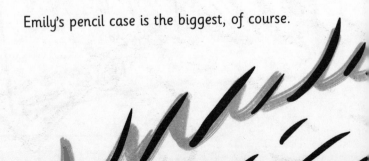

Mine is kind of funny. But Chloe's is

AMAZING.

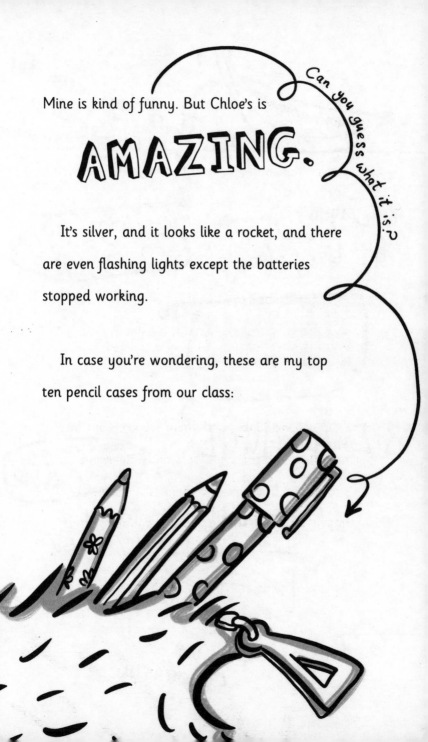

Can you guess what it is?

It's silver, and it looks like a rocket, and there are even flashing lights except the batteries stopped working.

In case you're wondering, these are my top ten pencil cases from our class:

10. There isn't a number ten so I've drawn a zip on a banana

9. Jayda's: bit lovey dovey →

8. Emily's: HUGE

7. Lily Ann's: from her skiing holiday

6. Tai's: not fancy but COLOURFUL

Anyway, Chloe and Emily were still busy drawing. So Notes unzipped Chloe's pencil case, rolled up the note, pushed it in, then zipped it all up again.

And we waited.

And waited.

Notes wandered across the desk to Emily's side, then curled up next to the cat pencil topper.

She stroked its funny plastic head as she watched Chloe, waiting, still waiting.

And then it was tidy-up time.

Emily stuffed all her pens and pencils back inside her fluffy pencil case. **(Notes sulked when the cat pencil topper went away.)**

But Chloe wasn't going anywhere near her pencil case, so she still hadn't found the note.

Notes yawned. She shlumped across the table, got her magic pencil. Then she doodled something on the desk in front of Chloe.

ticky tocky ticky tocky

But of course Chloe didn't have a clue. She couldn't see Notes, or her scribbles.

I wasn't going to wait any longer.

"Chloe," I whispered, "look in your pencil case."

"Why?" Chloe said.

I pointed at her pencil case, totally not being subtle any more.

"Just look," I said. "Please?"

"O-kay ..." she said.

Finally!

"But remember it's a secret, though," I said.

"A secret. Right."

She slid the zip, pulled out the note, unrolled it, read it, laughed.

And that was it.

She dropped Notes' note on the table and started getting changed for PE.

"Chloe?" I whispered. "Don't you want to see my secret friend?"

"I love your jokes, Molly-Moo. But maybe

after PE? Mr Stilton's gonna moan if we're slow."

Oh great. She thought I was just messing around.

Out the corner of my eye I saw Notes waving a note:

Ask if Chloe wants be secret friendling!

I was trying!

"Chloe?" I whispered, again.

"Yeah?" she said.

I looked over at Emily to check she wasn't listening. "If you met someone amazing," I said to Chloe, "... someone unbelievably magical ... someone tiny and secret and funny. Would you want to be her friend?"

She rolled her eyes. "What's this about?"

"Just answer!" I whispered. "Would you be her friend?"

"Fine," she said. "Yes. Why not?"

Down on the table, Notes did a happy somersault.

Here goes, I thought. *"Chloe,"* I whispered. *"Meet Notes!"*

CHAPTER TEN

"Notes!" said Mr Stilton, and I jumped higher than a kangaroo on a pogo stick.

Because, of course, I thought he meant Notes the witch.

Though I soon realised he didn't. He snatched up the paper note and scrunched it into his fist.

"More notes?!" he said. "Do I need to talk to your parents?"

"No! That's an old note," I lied. "It ... it fell out

of my pencil case. Didn't it, Chloe? Chloe?"

Chloe didn't answer. Didn't even look at me. She was staring at our table and her eyes were as big as ping-pong balls.

She was looking right at Notes. Notes, who was grinning and scribbling a messy note on the table.

"Chloe?" I said, again. "Isn't it an old note?"

"Old note," she agreed, still staring at Notes.

"See," I said with my teeth clenched in a nervous smile.

Mr Stilton mumbled something about "putting this much effort into school work".

But Emily was listening in now, and she pointed out the time, and Mr Stilton forgot about the note because we were really REALLY late for PE. (I wasn't sure if Emily was helping on purpose, or if she just didn't want to miss PE — but either way I was grateful.)

"Line up, worms!" Mr Stilton probably said (I can't exactly remember). "There's no time to get changed properly!"

Everyone lined up, but Chloe seemed to have forgotten how to move.

This was Chloe:

NOT BLINKING!!

So I led my super-stunned best friend into the line.

And I sort of expected my witchy friendling to come too.

Notes even picked up her magic pencil as if she planned on flying outside with us.

But she kept looking back at Emily's pencil case.

Which was odd.

Eventually she scribbled a quick message:

See friendlings soon.
Wants see Captain Purrkins.

"Captain who?!"

Huh?

There was no time to question it.

We walked in twos. Chloe didn't stay stunned for long.

"What. Was. That?!" she said.

"Keep your voice down! She's called Notes. She's our friend!"

"But what is she?!"

"She's a paper witch," I said.

"A paper witch, Molly?! A paper witch! Can you believe it?! A real witch, Molly! A real witch made of paper! How long have you known? Can she do magic? This is incredible, Molly. Incredible!"

"Shush!" I said, trying to look serious so she'd know to hush up. But inside I was grinning like this:

Because Notes *was* incredible. And what's
even more incredible was this – my plan was
working. Chloe was going to choose Dungfields. I
just knew it!

Wheeeeeep! Mr Stilton blew the metal

whistle which dangled around his bristly neck.

"One ball between two," he said. He pointed
at a damp bag of half-deflated footballs.
"Spread out, and practise your passes."

We chose the least mouldy ball and took it as
far away from Mr Stilton as possible.

← seriously old!

And at long last, I told Chloe all about meeting Notes, and about The Curse of Bony Parrot, and about getting told off by Mrs Banton. And I told her about the magic pencil and the secret writing.

And by the time I was done, Chloe was hopping up and down, too excited to kick straight.

"You wait till you meet her properly," I said. "She's so funny."

"I can't wait!" she said.

She didn't have to.

WHOOOOOSH! Notes zoomed past my ear.

She stopped in front of Chloe and gave her a

note.

I ran over to read it too (we're best friends so I can).

Dear friendling Chloe,
Sorrys for makings Chloe stare
and stare. Notes is now have two
friendlings! So wondrous! And Notes
wants is spending times with new
friendlings but Notes is busy with
beings in love with new petkins.
Notes promises soonish writings to
Chloe. OK? Byezees! Notes ♡

We were too busy reading to see Notes whoosh off again.

But then someone shouted, "Look!"

It was Owen (remember Owen? Owen's the one with the 5th best pencil case). He pointed at the sky.

"Look!" he shouted. "It's a ... It's ... Wha-what is it?!"

Something way up there was zooming about, making trails in the clouds.

Mr Stilton barely glanced up before bellowing,

"It's a plane. Back to your footballs!"

Rupa (owner of the 3rd best pencil case) squinted at the sky. "It's not a plane, Mr Stilton! Look, it's too small!" she said. "Plus it's drawing pictures!"

And she's right, it was.

Mr Stilton groaned. "Use your brains, people. It's called being very far away. It's probably one of those fancy stunt planes that can leave trails ... write messages ... that kind of thing. Can we please get on with the lesson!"

"B-but ..." said just about everybody (because this so obviously wasn't a plane).

But Mr Stilton was having none of it. "Enough!" he yelled. "I don't want to hear any more about clouds and planes and pictures!"

Chloe looked at me. I looked at Chloe.

"Is that ..." Chloe whispered.

I nodded. It was Notes. It had to be.

Notes seemed to be drawing a heart in the sky. And the heart seemed to have whiskers.

But what did it mean?

The whiskery heart soon puffed away, and Notes disappeared back inside.

We kicked the ball around a bit longer, waiting for Mr Stilton to ring the bell. And when he did, we were first in line.

Mr Stilton gave us a frowny look like how come you're so keen to get back to lessons?

Truth is we wanted to get back to Notes.

Anyway, I was at the front of the line, leading everyone back to class. But when I stepped through the door, I stopped dead still and just stared and stared.

Because all over the walls and ceiling and tables and chairs ... all over EVERYTHING ... were drawings of Emily's cat pencil topper.

And suddenly I got it. The heart, the whiskers, of course! Notes wanted that little plastic cat! *He* was Captain Purrkins!

I crossed my fingers and toes, hoping Notes had used her magic invisible pencil. I couldn't know for sure, but I guessed that **Mr Stilton + graffiti = bad news.**

Luckily, no one except Chloe looked bothered, so I figured they couldn't see it.

"What's happening?! What on Earth?!?" Chloe said, all breathless.

We stood there gawping, as the rest of the class shoved past.

I told Chloe about Emily's pencil topper.

"Makes sense," she said, which surprised me a bit.

"It does? How?" I said.

"Well, she's a witch, so she wants a witch's cat. Why don't you give her your cat pencil topper?"

I hadn't thought of that.

"Good thinking," I said.

Of course, then I'd only have six pencil toppers. But I could save up my pocket money for another one.

It was the perfect solution.

We found Notes sitting on the edge of the pen pot, resting her chin in her tiny hands.

"Psst! Notes!" I said.

She jolted upright.

"I've got something for you. If you want it," I said.

Chloe was already digging into my pencil case to get my cat pencil topper. She tossed it to me and I plonked it on the table in front of Notes.

"Ta-dah!" I whispered. "Will he do? Or is he a she?" I hadn't really thought about it.

Notes sighed. She was running out of room to write on the table so she got one of my felt tips and wrote on my hand.

Thankings, but no thankings. Notes is only wanting Captain Purrkins.

Chloe leaned in, whispering too. "Don't worry, Notes," she said. "It'll be OK."

And I smiled a tiny bit. Because even though
I was sad for Notes, I was happy too. Happy
that the three of us were friends. Happy that my
mission to make Chloe stay was working.

Chloe was right. It would all be OK, I thought.

How wrong was I!

CHAPTER ELEVEN

Tuesday was supposed to be Chloe's last day at Dungfields. But my plan to keep her here was going brilliantly. I just had to keep the fun times coming. This would be Chloe's day of fabulousness! A fantastic happy-fest! Easy, I thought, with Notes here to help.

But Notes was miserable.

Overnight she seemed to have gone from mopey-but-fun to just plain glum. She didn't want to come out of the pen pot. She didn't want to write. She didn't even want my pencil sharpenings.

Emily and Chloe sat either side of me, copying out today's spellings. In silence, of course. Always in silence. Mr Stilton loves silence. Chloe says he loves silence so much he'd marry it if he could.

Anyway, I grabbed a spare spelling sheet and wrote on the back. Then I passed it under the table to Emily.

Want to swap ~~Captain Purrkins~~ your cat pencil topper for one of mine?

No thanks.

Two of mine? No.

Three of mine?

No, it's my favourite.
Stop writing, I'm busy.

Four?   Five?

    Six?

Why won't you
answer?!

All seven?!?
Just think about it.

Urgh. Why did this have to be so hard? There
was no way Emily would change her mind. She
was so stubborn. So I wrote to Notes (and I
really shouldn't have).

Notes,
Sorry you're sad. But do you think you could
    pretend to be happy today? Even though
you're not.
                              Love from Molly x

(I'm not proud of myself. But I needed today to be all sparkly happy and glittery rainbows and non-stop super-fantastic, so Chloe would stay.)

Anyway, I put it in the pen pot and waited.

A little while later, she threw a note out in response.

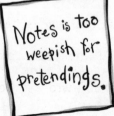

Notes is too weepish for pretendings.

Ohpleaseohpleaseohplease!!! For me?

(I may have panicked at this point.)

Eventually her little head popped out. She didn't smile, but she nodded.

I mouthed the words "thank you".

If I'm honest, I didn't think Notes could do it. I didn't think she could go from being the glummest glump in glumsville to being all whizzy and wonderful, but she totally did. I'm not even kidding.

This is what happened on **Chloe's Day of Fabulousness** ...

First, Notes stamped on Mr Stilton's head while he called the register (he didn't notice).

Blah blah blah blah...

Chloe had to hold her nose and mouth shut at the same time to stop giggling.

Next, Notes balanced on her flying pencil and danced a can-can all the way through Mrs Banton's dull assembly on "We can all try harder".

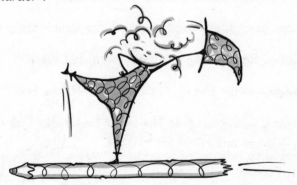

In English, Notes acted out the characters from our pirate stories. I almost said something

to her. Something like, "it's OK, you can stop now," or something like, "really, please stop," or something like, "I'm sorry" ...

But I didn't.

At break, Notes showed Chloe her loop-the-loop tricks. Chloe kept sneaking me little secret grins. I had to fake-grin back because I wasn't feeling overly grinny. (It's really hard to feel grinny and guilty at the same time.) But Chloe looked so ridiculously happy. It was working.

After that, Notes slept. I couldn't blame her really. She'd been so crazy-busy acting happy.

I put a little pile
of multicoloured
sharpenings in the pen
pot. Maybe she'd eat them
when she woke up, I thought.

Just before lunch, Notes climbed out of the
pen pot, ignoring the sharpenings. She looked so
tired, but she tried to hide it. She smiled at Chloe
and gave her a big thumbs-up.

All through lunch she wrote jokes on leaves in
the Secret Spot. You had to turn them over for
the funny bits.

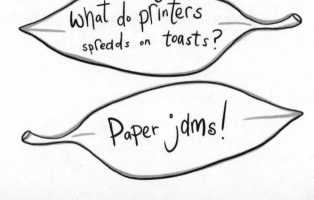

What do printers spredds on toasts?

Paper jams!

Chloe laughed and laughed, and I laughed too (even though I didn't feel like it at all).

Then, for the whole of the afternoon, Notes did acrobatics in class. She somersaulted from chair to chair. She did cartwheels across the table. She walked on her hands, right the way across Mr Stilton's desk. She catapulted herself across the room on rulers. She was absolutely as fun as I'd hoped. Funner in fact.

The FUNNEST Scribble Witch EVER.

And she did it all for me, even when she was miserable. All to help me make Chloe stay.

Which made it doubly horrible when Chloe

gave me the worst of all possible notes:

Molly,

I have had the most crazymazing (new word because I'm excited) last day! Thanks for giving me smashwhopping (another new word - ha ha!) memories. And thanks for introducing me to Notes. She's so beyond cool. I'm going to miss you both so much!

Love Chloe x

"What?!" I said. "You're going to miss us? You're still leaving? Even though Notes is here? Even though she's insanely ridiculously fun?!"

Chloe kind of looked like I'd walloped her, which I swear I hadn't. I was just really disappointed, and she was really shocked, and the whole thing felt really rubbish.

"I'm sorry, Molly," she said. "It's not up to me."

"But if you tell your mum you really, really want to stay ..."

She shook her head. "It's too late. Mum signed letters and stuff."

So that was that. There was nothing I could do. She was going.

I wanted to cry. Actually, what I really wanted to do was throw a **humungous strop** like one of the little kids in Reception. I wanted to yell and shove and lie on my back and drum my heels into the ground.

But I didn't. Because:

1. I'd look like a total custard-brain.

2. If this really was Chloe's last day (which it turns out, it was) then I didn't want to ruin it.

Chloe's dad got to the school gate before my mum that afternoon. Notes sat on my shoulder hugging my hair and we watched Chloe leave Dungfields. And we didn't stop waving until she was totally out of sight.

"Sorry, Notes," I whispered. *"It was all for nothing."*

I'd been a rubbish friend to Notes.

She had her own problems. I shouldn't have asked her to pretend to be happy. It wasn't fair.

I hoped maybe she'd want to go home with me and sleep in my pencil case or something. But when I asked her she shook her head. Then she flew off, back into school.

So I didn't have a chance to be a better friend.

Or, more like, I did have the chance.

I had it, and I missed it.

CHAPTER TWELVE

Wednesday was always going to be a stinker
of a day.

1. It was my first day without Chloe.
And yeah, she'd had days off sick and
stuff, but this was different. She was
NEVER coming back to Dungfields. Never
ever.

2. Wednesday is spellings day, and
I'd been a bit too busy to think about
spellings.

Emily was at the front of the line waiting
to go into class. And the first thing she said to
me was, "I've learnt all my spellings. Bet you
haven't."

She was right. I hadn't.

I stared at my shiny shoes, toeing the gravel. I
couldn't be bothered to argue.

Funny thing is, when I didn't argue, Emily
didn't really know what to do.

"Well, did you?" she said eventually.

"Nope," I said.

I could feel her watching me even though I wasn't looking at her. And then she did a very un-Emily type thing. She sighed, then she pulled a notebook from her bag, and she gave it to me.

"Look at these," she said. "You may as well practise while we wait to go in."

"Thanks," I said.

And that's the weird thing about Emily. You think she's all showy-offy (and she is) but sometimes she just surprises you.

Anyway, I spent a few minutes looking at the spellings and then beardy Stilton let us in.

Class wasn't the same without Chloe. I hated seeing her locker all empty and I hated that her birthday date was gone from the birthday display. And I really hated that no one else even seemed to notice.

At least I'd still got Notes to keep me company though.

"Notes!" I hissed. I looked in the pen pot. "You there?"

I had something for her. I'd made it before school. It was a tiny card to say sorry. And it really was tiny. I had to use a magnifying glass and it wasn't easy but she deserved it.

I wanted to give it to her straight away. I wanted to show her I could be a great friend. **Starting from now.**

But she wasn't in the pen pot.

And then I noticed her drawings had gone. There were no more sentences scribbled across the table, no more cat doodles across the ceiling and walls.

A fluttery sicky feeling bubbled inside me.

Had Notes cleaned it all away? Had it faded overnight? Maybe that was how the magic worked. Otherwise Notes would run out of places to write pretty quickly, right? Yep, I thought. That was definitely it.

But what if I was wrong?

What if she was gone too?! First Chloe, now Notes. They couldn't both leave me, could they?!

I dropped the little card into the pen pot.

Where was she?!

"Settle down, grottlings!" Mr Stilton said

(and OK, I admit it, he might not have actually said grottlings but he definitely thought it).

He sipped his stinky coffee then called the register.

"Mustafa?"
"Here, Mr Stilton."

"Lily Ann?"
"Here, Mr Stilton."

"Molly?"
"Here, Mr Stilton."

And then he called out, "Chloe? Chloe Trout?" before remembering she'd gone.

And that was it. That's all it took. My eyes started burning and welling up and everything was leaking and snuffly and AWFUL.

I took my mini notebook from my pencil case and tore out a page.

Notes,
please
come back.

I crumpled it into the pen pot too, and hoped.

I watched Mr Stilton through **BLURRY EYES.**
Like I was looking through smudged glass. His
fuzzy shape pointed at the board as he gave
out instructions. I have to admit I wasn't really
listening by this point.

He might have been
telling us how to train
dragons, or steal
the crown jewels.
I wouldn't have
noticed.

Someone tapped me on the shoulder. I spun round, thinking maybe Notes would be there, hovering beside me. She wasn't.

"*Emily?!*" I whispered.

She glared at me, warning me to be quiet. Then she slid something in front of me on the table.

Captain Purrkins.

Folded beneath him was a note.

You can have it. Hope it cheers you up.

I gawped at her. A proper jaw-drop gawp.

She shrugged like it was no big deal. But it
was a big deal.

Thank you
sooooo
much!!!

Again, she shrugged. But this time the corner
of her mouth curled up a teensy bit. Just the
tiniest, secret smile, and then it was gone.

So that was a surprise.

And it got me wondering if Emily would be different, now that it wasn't her against me and Chloe. Maybe showing off had been her way of saying "I don't need you two – I'm already brilliant on my own ..." which was hopeful (because I liked the idea of a non-showy-offy Emily) but also sad (because we made her that way).

Anyway, I was grateful for Captain Purrkins. Though now I was more desperate than ever to see Notes (and more scared than ever that she might not come back).

I wiped my eyes (and nose – don't tell anyone) on my sleeve and tried to pay attention to Mr Stilton. Notes was bound to be back by break time.

Except she wasn't. In fact, by break time I was starting to wonder if I'd imagined her.

Emily offered to help me learn the spellings again, but I couldn't concentrate. So we said we'd do it at lunchtime, because spelling tests are always in the afternoon (or so we thought).

Instead, I went to the Secret Spot. I wanted to see if Notes' leafy messages were still there. I wanted proof she was real.

But there was no proof.

Just like in class, everything was as it always had been. It was as though Notes had never existed.

At least things couldn't get any worse, I told myself.

Now, here's some advice:

NEVER THINK THINGS CAN'T GET ANY WORSE.

If you think you're going to think it, just go lalalalala until you think something else instead. Things do sometimes get worse.

For example, you could get back to class after break and find out you have a *spelling test* straight away instead of after lunch. Which is what happened.

And maybe you're thinking what's the big deal? This is the big deal: **if you get less than twelve out of twenty you don't get to do choosing time on Friday.**

And choosing time is the best bit of the week because (in case you didn't guess) you can choose what to do. Which in mine and Chloe's case is always **drawing.**

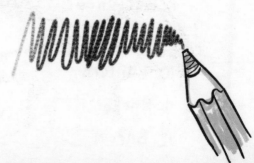

Anyway, normally I get around thirteen.

Twelve is my lowest. But this week I was worried.

Mr Stilton read the spellings out one by one,

and I tried really hard to remember them.

1. Pirate
2. Parrot
3. Dubloons
4. Eyeland
5. Ship
6. Captain
7. Rifle
8. Buckanear
9. Cutless
10. Lantern
11. Anchor
12. Barrel
13. Plank
14. Sailer
15. Ceg
16. Harber
17. Plunder
18. Booty
19. Ors
20.

I knew I'd got loads of them wrong, but maybe if I got the last one right it'd all be OK.

And then he said it ... the one word I absolutely definitely could not spell.

Tresher ... trejur ... Yeah. **That one.**

Just my luck, I thought. My worst Wednesday had gone from bad to really bad to oh so bad to so so SO bad. There was no hope. I was going to fail.

Defeated, I doodled on my test sheet, thinking of Notes, thinking I'd never see her again. I put down my pencil and stared gloomily out of the half-open window. And that's when I saw it.

A paper plane. And riding on the plane was my favourite ever witchy.

It came soaring into class, over everyone's heads. But because everyone was busy with spellings, no one saw. Not even Mr Stilton. It circled round the room then landed in front of me.

And written on the outside was one word:

Treasure

"*You came back!*" I whispered to Notes.

CHAPTER THIRTEEN

Everyone was checking through their spellings, which meant no one noticed the whacking great grin on my face.

She pointed at question twenty on my list and I quickly scribbled down the answer, but — honestly — I hardly cared about the spellings any more. **Notes was back!!**

She pushed the plane towards me.

I couldn't believe it. A note from Chloe! It was definitely her writing. I opened it up and read.

Dear Molly,

Treasure! That's the word you were trying to spell on Monday, right? It just popped into my head. And talking of treasure, Notes is kind of like our treasure, isn't she! Way better than the pirate kind! She's so clever, with the super-speedy invisible writing and the flying! I wonder if she can do anything else? I bet she can. I bet she can do loads of magic.

Also, WHY DIDN'T YOU TELL ME ABOUT YOUR AMAZING PLAN?! It's so cool that Notes can fly messages between Dungfields and Juniper's! Literally the best news ever!!

from your best friend,
                    Chloe xx

P.S. I'm sitting next to a girl called Daffodil who keeps telling really bad jokes.

P.P.S Why don't the other numbers like zero?? Because zero is so noughty! Get it?!

I looked at Notes, not even knowing what to say.

I wasn't the clever one, Notes was.

"You can really fly messages between me and Chloe?" I whispered. "So we can still write notes in class?"

She leaned her head on one side, frowning. Then she picked up her magic pencil.

Notes is confusled.
Notes is been thinkings about flyings from Dungpoop to Lady Jupiter for agings and agings! Ever since Chloe becomed Notes' friendling!
Why Molly has WOW face?!?

I shook my head. "Because ... You're brilliant!

So brilliant. You have no idea how very

amazingly awesomely brilliant

you are!"

She'd been planning to fly letters from school

to school all along! Dungfields to Lady Juniper's

... Lady Juniper's to Dungfields. And all along

she thought it was obvious.

She was prepared to do all that for me and

Chloe.

"So that's where you've been all morning?

Looking after Chloe at her new school?" I said.

She grinned and nodded.

"So you're not mad at me?" I said.

She frowned, confused, like it hadn't even occurred to her that I'd been a horrible terrible friend.

Then I remembered the "sorry" card.

"Oh!" I said. "This is for you."

I picked it out of the pen pot and gave it to her. She read it, smiling at my drawing of Captain Purrkins. Then she hugged it to her tummy.

Which then reminded me ... "Oh – oh - oh! Captain Purrkins!"

I put him in front of Notes.

Her mouth fell open. Her fingers spread wide like tiny starbursts. And I swear I saw doodly hearts in her eyes.

"He's yours," I said.

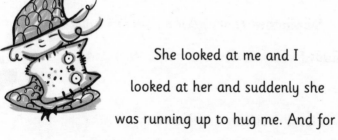

She looked at me and I
looked at her and suddenly she
was running up to hug me. And for
some reason she hugged my nose, which
was a bit odd but also OK. Then she jumped
down and put Captain Purrkins on the end of her
magic pencil.

So that's it. That's how my worst Wednesday turned into my most wonderful Wednesday.

Notes couldn't have been happier now she had Captain Purrkins. And seeing her happy made me super-happy too.

All there was left to do was write back to Chloe. I couldn't do it straight away but at lunchtime I snuck out my pencil case and some paper.

I ate lunch with Emily (no leaky yoghurt – yippee!). And when she went to her bassoon lesson I went and hid in the Secret Spot.

Notes came too, and we sat together, and I
wrote the best note I'd written in a long time.

Dear Chloe,

I got your letter!
How amazing is this?!
I hope you're making loads of friends.
That zero joke is ~~hilairyus~~ so funny!
It's weird without you but I think I'll be OK.
Writing makes it feel like you're still kind
of here!

Hugest hugs!

From your best friend Molly
XxXx

P.S. Notes is our treasure for definite! But
I don't think she can do any other magic.

P.P.S. Maybe though. You never
know with Notes...

Read on for more
SCRIBBLE WITCH
adventures in book 2:

magical Muddles

Hello,

Molly here. I'm pretty down in
the dumps now Chloe's moved
school and has loads of new
friends. And what's worse, she's
entered the Inter-School Spelling
Championship! But if Chloe can
be all no-big-deal about it, then
I will too. Except for the fact I
absolutely HATE spelling tests ...

Molly x

Hizees!
Remember Me?
I is Notes, secret paper witchy.
Molly is sads and jealousings that
her bestest friendling Chloe
looooves her new school.
So I does wondrous
helpings to find Molly
brand-new splendid friendling and
Maybeez help with spelling
muddles alongs the way!
Back soons!
Notes
x

How to draw:
SCRIBBLE
WITCH

★ start with these basic shapes

1.
2.
3.
4.
5.
6.
7.
8.

Ta-da!

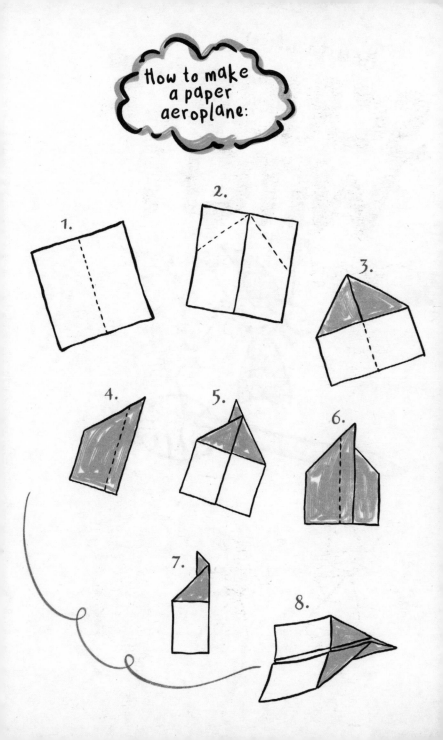

How to make
a paper
aeroplane:

1.

2.

3.

4.

5.

6.

7.

8.